This edition is published and distributed
exclusively by Discovery Toys, Inc.,
Martinez, CA

First published in 1989 by
Walker Books, Ltd.,
London

Printed in Hong Kong

ISBN 0-939979-28-4

MY MOM IS FANTASTIC!

DISCOVERY TOYS, INC.

My mom is fantastic.

She's a brilliant artist . . .

and she can balance
on a tightrope . . .

and she can fix anything . . .

and she tells the most
exciting stories . . .

and she's a fantastic gardener . . .

and she can swim like a fish . . .

and she can do amazing
stunts on a bike . . .

and she can knit anything . . .

and she can tame wild animals . . .

and she makes the best
parties in the world.

It's great to have
a mom like mine.

She's fantastic!